www.mascotbooks.com

Football Freddie & Fumble the Dog: Gameday in Chicago

For more information, please contact:
Mascot Books
620 Herndon Parkway #320
Herndon, VA 20170
info@mascotbooks.com

Library of Congress Control Number: 2019904771

CPSIA Code: PRT0719A
ISBN-13: 978-1-64543-012-4

Printed in the United States of America

FOOTBALL FREDDIE
& FUMBLE THE DOG

Gameday in Chicago

THE MAGNIFICENT MILE

Marnie Schneider
Jonathan Witten

Illustrated by
Agus Prajogo

*Dedicated to Chicago
fans everywhere.*

BEAR DOWN!

Hi! My name's **Freddie**, and this is my trusty companion **Fumble**. We're on our way to Soldier Field to watch the Bears play today, or as they say here, "Da Bears"!

Other sights near Millennium Park include the Shedd Aquarium and the Adler Planetarium.

First though, my friend Pilar will show us around some of the sights here in Chicago. She's a native Chicagoan and loves her city! Our first stop is **Millennium Park**! Look at all the people walking around and taking in the sights. Millennium Park has won lots of awards for its accessibility and design. Pilar shows us a sculpture called "Cloud Gate." Fumble really likes how shiny it is!

Northwestern University

Loyola University

Other nicknames for Chicago are "The City of Broad Shoulders," "My Kind of Town," and "The Second City."

90

DePaul University

The Art Institute of Chicago

University of Illinois at Chicago

The University of Chicago

Chicago is known as the **"Windy City"** for all the wind that comes off Lake Michigan. Some say it's also because of all the politicians in the city. Make sure you're bundled up, Fumble—we don't want to catch a cold and miss the game today!

There are so many great colleges here in Chicago. One that's not on this map is the Second City Comedy Improv. Pilar thinks you'd fit in well there, Fumble. You're such a natural comedian!

FREE SOCIETY IS NOT AND
SHALL NOT BE A FAILURE

Abraham Lincoln
Chicago, Dec. 10, 1856

Chicago is the biggest city in the state of Illinois. One of the most famous people from Illinois is **Abraham Lincoln**! There's a statue of him here in Chicago's Lincoln Square. Even though he wasn't born in Illinois, he lived here and served as a U.S. House of Representatives member for Illinois before being elected president.

Abraham Lincoln was the president all through the American Civil War and signed the **Emancipation Proclamation**. Pilar wants to be just like him when she's older!

Another thing Chicago is known for is its skyscrapers! The very first skyscraper in the world was built here, all the way back in 1885. The **Willis Tower**, which used to be called the Sears Tower, was the tallest skyscraper in the world for 25 years.

Three of the world's tallest skyscrapers—the Willis Tower, the John Hancock Building, and the Aon Center—are located in Chicago.

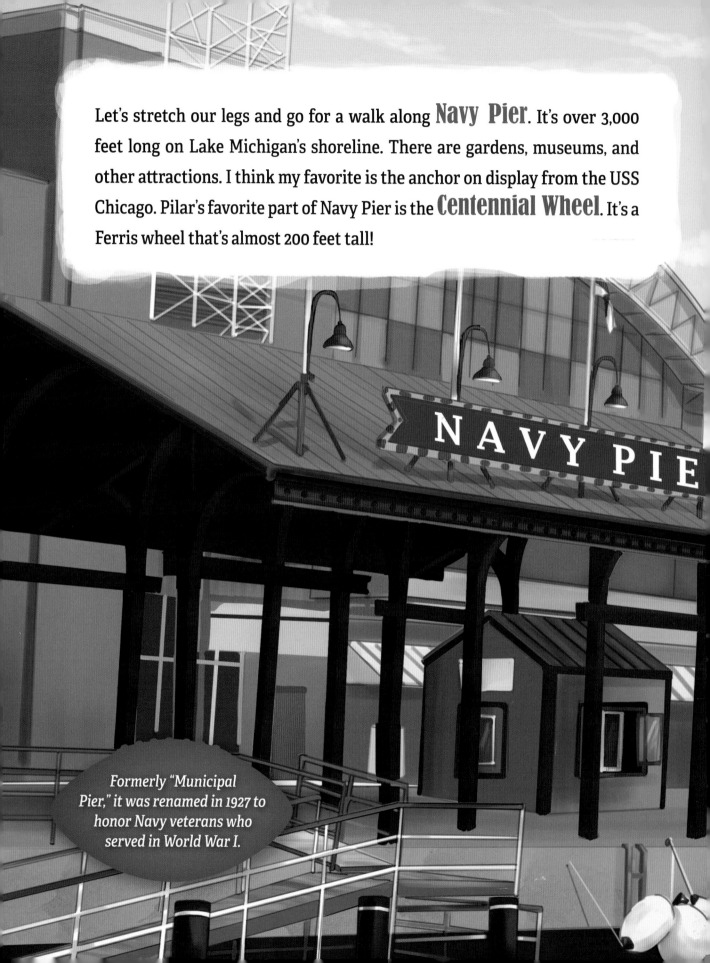

Let's stretch our legs and go for a walk along **Navy Pier**. It's over 3,000 feet long on Lake Michigan's shoreline. There are gardens, museums, and other attractions. I think my favorite is the anchor on display from the USS Chicago. Pilar's favorite part of Navy Pier is the **Centennial Wheel**. It's a Ferris wheel that's almost 200 feet tall!

Formerly "Municipal Pier," it was renamed in 1927 to honor Navy veterans who served in World War I.

Star of Chicago

Time to do a little shopping! There's no better place for it than along Chicago's **Magnificent Mile**. This mile-long stretch in Chicago's downtown has tons of luxury stores and fine dining. Pilar likes to come here to window shop and try on the latest fashions. Looking good, Fumble!

Famous Chicago blues musicians include Muddy Waters, Howlin' Wolf, Bo Diddley, and Willie Dixon.

The **Art Institute of Chicago** is one of the oldest and largest museums in the United States. It has over 300,000 works of art and 30 special exhibitions! This one is called *A Sunday Afternoon on the Island of La Grande Jatte* by Georges Seurat. This is what they did on Sundays before football, Fumble! Let's take a picture, Pilar. It'll look great on my Instagram feed!

The **Garfield Park Conservatory** is one of the largest conservatories in the United States. It is beautiful and full of many plants, some of which are very unique. It's a great place to visit when it's cold outside!

Pilar's favorite room here is the **Palm Room**. There are over seven dozen different types of palm trees here! It takes so much work and care to grow palm trees—the gardeners here are truly amazing!

It's time to eat! We'll need to keep our strength up in order to cheer for the home team all through the game. Lucky for us, there's no shortage of great food here in Chicago. Pilar brought us some **Chicago-style hot dogs** to try—just look at all the toppings on them, Fumble! Other famous foods here in Chicago are **Chicago-style deep dish pizza** and **Chicago mix popcorn**. Let's dig in before paying our respects at the Soldier Field mural!

SOLDIER FIELD
DEDICATED TO THE DEFENDERS OF OUR LIBERTY

Soldier Field opened in 1924 and serves as a memorial to U.S. soldiers who died in combat.

It's **game time**! People from Chicago are so dedicated to their sports teams—not just for their football team, but their baseball, basketball, and hockey teams. Isn't it great to see so many people out here on gameday to cheer on their team? Fans are the best, whether you're rooting for the Bears, the Cubs, the Bulls, the Sox, or the Blackhawks! **Go Chicago!**

The Chicago Bears's colors are navy blue and orange.

The Chicago Bears are one of the oldest teams in the National Football League—they were founded all the way back in 1920! Look down there, Fumble. Their quarterback made a short pass and now they've run the football all the way to the **endzone**. Pilar is jumping up and down with excitement—that means six points for the Bears!

All NFL games have seven different officials on the field to make sure everyone plays by the rules.

The home team is still in the lead at **halftime**, but we need to keep up the defense. We need to keep our lead!

For halftime, they're doing something special. Chicago's firefighters and police officers are helping honor George Stanley Halas, the founder of the team! He's one of Pilar's role models—she says that he always had great words of wisdom like, "No one who ever gave his best regretted it."

DA BEARS!

George Stanley Halas was also known as "Papa Bear" and "Mr. Everything" by Bears fans.

We did it! The Bears held them off to win the game!

Soon we'll be doing the Super Bowl Shuffle again!

George Allen helped popularize the famous "Nickel Defense" during his time with the Bears.

It's been another great day here in Chicago, Fumble. We need to remember to write a thank-you letter to Pilar for showing us around her city.

XOXO *(that's football language),*
— **Football Freddie and Fumble the Dog**

About the Authors

A Pennsylvania native and Penn State graduate (WE ARE!), Marnie's life has been driven by sports. Her grandfather, Leonard Tose, was a longtime member of the "club" as the owner of the Philadelphia Eagles. He was also the founder of the Ronald McDonald House and helped build NFL Films. From him, Marnie learned the importance of family, sports, and charity. Her series, *Football Freddie and Fumble the Dog* is her way of giving back to the many great football communities across the nation.

Jonathan Witten is the third generation in a long line of football fans. Diagnosed with neuroblastoma cancer at a young age and unable to walk or talk until age 5, he went on to play varsity football and is currently attending college. He loves watching football with his younger brother and sister. His grandmother, Susan T. Spencer, was the

Leonard Tose and the young author.

first woman in pro football to be the vice president, legal counsel, and acting general manager. She did all of this at the Philadelphia Eagles. She's the author of *Briefcase Essentials* and co-author of *Gameday in Philadelphia*, the first book in the Football Freddie series. Susan also runs a very successful nonprofit called A Level Playing Field, which helps kids play sports safely.

Chicago Facts:

Motto
Urbs in Horto
(City in a Garden)

Flag

Year of Establishment
1837

Nicknames
Windy City, City of Big Shoulders,
My Kind of Town, The Second City

Dedicated to my mom Susan Tose Spencer.

The first ever female GM, Legal Counsel,
and VP of a pro football club!